Bo and the School Bully

by Elliott Smith
illustrated by Subi Bosa

Cicely Lewis, Executive Editor

Lerner Publications ◆ Minneapolis

A Letter from Cicely Lewis

Dear Reader,

This series is about a boy named Bo and his grandfather in the barbershop called the Buzz. The barbershop has always been the hub of the Black community. In a world where Black voices are often silenced, it is a place where these voices can be heard.

I created the Read Woke challenge for my students so they can read books that reflect the diversity of the world. I hope you see the real-life beauty, richness, and joy of Black culture shine through these pages.

—Cicely Lewis, Executive Editor

TABLE OF CONTENTS

Bo's World

Hi, I'm Bo. I like basketball,
science, and flying in airplanes.
This is my grandpa, Roger.
I call him Pop-Pop.

We live upstairs from the Buzz. It's the barbershop Pop-Pop owns.

I like hanging out with my friends Silas, Shawn, and Zuri.

CHAPTER 1
The Threat

"Don't forget to bring *MegaQuest 2!*"
Bo said. It was lunchtime, and he and
Silas were planning a sleepover for
the weekend. Suddenly, the cafeteria
got quiet. Everyone knew what this
meant: Quincy was there.

Quincy was the tallest, meanest kid
in the grade. He terrorized a different
kid every day. No one was safe. And
today, a shadow landed on Bo and
Silas's table. Bo's heart raced.

"Give me your dessert," Quincy said to Silas.

Silas started to hand Quincy his cookies, his eyes wide.

"Hey! Leave him alone!" Bo said. The kids in the cafeteria all gasped. No one ever talked back to Quincy.

"What are you going to do about it?" Quincy asked. He cracked his knuckles. It sounded like fireworks.

Bo looked around for some help, but everyone looked away. He gulped. "Uh . . . uh . . ." he muttered.

"Now you have to bring me something extra special," Quincy growled. "And you better have it on Monday. *Or else.*"

11

Quincy stomped away and sat at the empty table where he always ate lunch.

"Thanks, Bo," Silas said. "But now what are you going to do?"

Bo was shaking. "Maybe I'll tell Pop-Pop I'm sick on Monday."

CHAPTER 2
Good Advice

Bo was refilling the aftershave bottles at the Buzz on Sunday. His stomach flipped and flopped. What would he do about Quincy? Run? Hide? Fight?

"Pop-Pop, how do you stop a bully?" he asked. "I helped one of my friends, and now the bully is after me."

15

Pop-Pop's friends Floyd and Clyde chimed in from the back of the shop. "You should give him a good kick in the leg!" Floyd said. "Let me show you my karate moves."

"No, no. You should run as fast as you can—you're small," a laughing Clyde said.

17

"Y'all be quiet," Pop-Pop said. He turned to Bo. "I'm proud of you for standing up for your friend. You know, bullies can get to be that way because they're scared. They often have something tough going on."

19

Pop-Pop pointed at the picture of John Lewis on the wall. "John Lewis believed that love would win over hate. Try being nice to your bully. And if that doesn't work, call in a teacher. Tell them what's going on."

"Thanks, Pop-Pop," Bo said. He knew it was good advice. But still—Pop-Pop didn't know what Quincy was like.

Bo sighed. Tomorrow would be a long day.

CHAPTER 3
Showdown

Normally, Bo was excited for lunch. But when the bell rang on Monday, he felt sick.

It seemed like the whole grade was watching Bo and Silas eat. Then Quincy's loud footsteps approached Bo's table.

"Well?" Quincy snarled. "Did you bring something? Or should I hurt you?"

Suddenly, Bo didn't feel scared. "I did bring you something. Something great. But you only get it if you eat with us."

Quincy blinked. No one had ever asked Quincy to sit with them. "Uh, okay . . ." he said quietly. He sat next to Silas, who slid over a few inches.

25

26

"I brought my Pop-Pop's magical homemade banana pudding," Bo said. "He says it tastes best when eaten with friends."

Bo gave containers to Quincy and Silas.

"I don't have any friends here," Quincy said quietly. "When I moved, I left all my friends behind."

"You can be friends with us now,"
Bo said. "As long as you start being
nice to people."

"I'm sorry for being mean,"
Quincy said. He put a big spoonful
of Pop-Pop's banana pudding in
his mouth. "Wow! This pudding
tastes great!"

The boys talked and laughed through lunch. It turned out Quincy was pretty funny. And just like that, Bo and Silas had a new friend.

About the Author

Elliott Smith has been writing stories ever since he was a kid. This love of writing led him first to a career as a sports reporter. Now, he has written more than 40 children's books, both fiction and nonfiction. Smith lives just outside Washington, DC, with his wife and two children. He loves watching movies, playing basketball with his kids, and adding to his collection of Pittsburgh Steelers memorabilia.

About the Illustrator

As a child, Subi Bosa drew pictures all the time, in every room of the house—sometimes on the walls. His mother still tells everyone, "He knew how to draw before he could properly hold a pencil." In 2020, Subi was awarded a Mo Siewcharran Prize for Illustration. Subi lives in Cape Town, South Africa, creating picture books, comics, and graphic novels.

Lerner Publications Company
An imprint of Lerner Publishing Group, Inc.
241 First Avenue North
Minneapolis, MN 55401 USA

For reading levels and more information, look up this title at www.lernerbooks.com.

Main body text set in Mikado 24/41. Typeface provided by Hannes von Doehren.

Library of Congress Cataloging-in-Publication Data

Names: Smith, Elliott, 1976- author. | Bosa, Subi, illustrator.
Title: Bo and the school bully / by Elliott Smith ; illustrated by Subi Bosa.
Description: Minneapolis : Lerner Publications, [2023] | Series: Bo at the Buzz
   (Read woke chapter books) | Audience: Ages 6-9. | Audience: Grades 2-3. |
   Summary: When Bo stands up to a bully, he finds himself in the spotlight, but
   with Pop-Pop's help Bo defuses the situation and makes a new friend.
Identifiers: LCCN 2022011589 (print) | LCCN 2022011590
   (ebook) | ISBN 9781728476148 (lib. bdg.) | ISBN 9781728486284 (pbk.) |
   ISBN 9781728481517 (eb pdf)
Subjects: CYAC: Bullies—Fiction. | Friendship—Fiction. | African Americans—
   Fiction. | LCGFT: Fiction.
Classification: LCC PZ7.1.S626 Bor 2023 (print) | LCC PZ7.1.S626 (ebook) | DDC
   [Fic]—dc23

LC record available at https://lccn.loc.gov/2022011589
LC ebook record available at https://lccn.loc.gov/2022011590

Manufactured in the United States of America
1 - CG - 12/15/22